Contents

1

Introduction

Angina pectoris, or angina for short, is chest discomfort that occurs when the heart doesn't get enough oxygen. It can feel like pressure, squeezing, or pain in the chest. Angina can be stable, occurring chronically in people with coronary blockages, particularly during exercise or exertion. New or worsening angina is considered unstable angina and can progress to a heart attack.

Chapter one

What Is Angina?

Angina is a symptom that occurs when there is a problem with the flow of blood to the heart. The heart is a constantly working muscle that requires a great deal of oxygen and energy to function. Blood is supplied to the heart by the coronary arteries.

Any impairment of the supply of blood from the coronary arteries, such as in coronary atherosclerosis, can lead to chest discomfort, which is classically described as a dull pressure in the center of the chest that may radiate to the arm or jaw.

Types of Angina

Angina is classified as either stable or unstable. Stable angina is chronic chest pain that occurs with exertion and reliably improves with rest. It's usually experienced when the heart works harder and requires more blood and oxygen, such as during exercise or emotional stress. Other triggers include eating a heavy meal or extremes of temperature.

With exertion, the heart rate increases, and the heart pumps more forcefully to supply blood to the body, thus requiring a greater demand for oxygen. However, a blockage in the coronary arteries limits the amount of blood supply to the heart.

Unstable angina, on the other hand, is new angina, which occurs at rest or has become more frequent, longer-lasting, or severe. Unstable angina is considered a type of acute coronary syndrome. It's a medical emergency since it can progress to a heart attack and requires hospitalization for evaluation and treatment.

Angina can also be classified according to its causes. It usually is caused by atherosclerosis, a hardening and blockage of the artieries caused by a buildup of cholesterol plaques. Other types of angina are:

Microvascular angina, due to blockages of the small blood vessels of the heart that can't be visualized. It also may be caused by spasms in the microvasculature.

Variant angina, also known as Prinzmetal angina, is due to vasospasm, or a sudden temporary constriction, of a coronary artery. It typically occurs when a person is at rest. This classically occurs in the early morning hours and can be triggered by stress, cold, smoking, and certain medications such as nonsteroidal anti-inflammatory drugs (NSAIDs), and cocaine.

Angina Symptoms

Most people associate chest pain with blockages in the heart. However, people with angina may not ever have pain. They may instead describe a tightness, pressure, or squeezing sensation that isn't necessarily painful.

Angina is often described as a dull feeling in the area under the breastbone (sternum), though it's difficult to locate the precise position. The discomfort can radiate up to the neck, arms, upper abdomen, back, or jaw. Shortness of breath is another common symptom. Other symptoms can include the following:

Nausea

Light-headedness

Numbness

Palpitations

Epigastric discomfort (discomfort at the upper abdomen just below the ribs)

Sweating

Angina typically lasts for a few minutes, gradually increasing in severity before dissipating with rest.

Angina in Females

While chest pain is the most common symptom of angina regardless of sex, people assigned female at birth are more likely to have nonclassic symptoms. This can make the diagnosis more challenging and is one potential contributor to disparities in heart disease diagnosis and management in women.

Angina Treatments

Once a diagnosis of chronic, stable angina is made, the treatment plan includes lifestyle changes and medications to alleviate symptoms and prevent complications such as heart attack and death. Cardiac rehab is a supervised program for people diagnosed with heart disease that provides education, exercise prescription, and tailored advice on managing your condition.

Lifestyle Changes

The following lifestyle changes are recommended for heart health and to prevent future cardiovascular events in those with or without heart disease:

Getting regular physical exercise:

The American Heart Association recommends at least 150 minutes of moderate-intensity exercise per week. Cardiac rehab can help determine an appropriate exercise prescription and instructions.

Eating a heart-healthy diet:

This diet is rich in vegetables, fruits, whole grains, legumes, and fish and is low in processed foods, sodium, and trans fats

Medications for Angina

Medications to treat angina include:

Aspirin, an antiplatelet medication that helps thin the blood

Statins to lower cholesterol

Beta-blockers to slow heart rate and decrease workload on the heart

Calcium channel blockers decrease stress on the heart by lowering heart rate and blood pressure

Angiotensin converting enzyme (ACE) inhibitors to decrease blood pressure

Nitrates to relax blood vessels

Ranolazine to relaxes the heart muscle

Procedures

In some cases, such as if symptoms are affecting daily life significantly despite optimal medication regimen, your cardiologist may recommend revascularization to restore blood flow to the heart. This can be achieved through stenting or surgery.

Stenting is performed during a procedure called coronary angioplasty to open blocked coronary arteries. During this procedure, a cardiologist uses balloon-tipped catheters under X-ray guidance to reach the coronary arteries, open up the blockage, and place a stent, a flexible tube.

In certain cases, surgery is preferred. This is done with coronary artery bypass grafting (CABG). A cardiothoracic surgery will harvest a blood vessel (typically a vein from the leg) and use it to bypass the blockage in the heart.

What Causes Angina?

Angina is caused by anything that impedes blood flow to the heart muscle. Most commonly this is from atherosclerosis, or cholesterol plaques. However, other causes of angina include:

Congenital coronary malformations (coronary arteries with abnormalities since birth)

Coronary vasospasm, a narrowing of the arteries due to blood contracting persistently (Prinzmetal's angina)

Problems with the small blood vessels bringing oxygenated blood to the heart (microvascular angina)

Risk Factors for Angina

Angina is most often caused by atherosclerotic coronary artery disease, which is the most common form of cardiovascular disease. Risk factors include certain medical conditions and lifestyle factors:

High cholesterol

High blood pressure

Diabetes

Having obesity

Chronic kidney disease

Certain female-specific risk factors such as preeclampsia, early menopause, polycystic ovary syndrome (PCOS)

Family history of heart attack, especially at a young age

Smoking

Sedentary lifestyle

How Is Angina Diagnosed?

There are many potential causes of chest pain, some of which are benign while others may be life threatening. So it's important to receive a proper diagnosis. Your healthcare provider may have suspicion for angina based on your description of chest pain and order diagnostic tests. Tests to diagnose angina include:

Electrocardiogram (ECG or EKG)

Stress test, such as exercise stress test, stress echocardiogram, myocardial perfusion imaging (nuclear stress test)

Imaging tests such as echocardiogram, coronary computed tomography angiography (CTA)

Coronary angiography, an invasive test in which cardiologists use catheters, X-rays and contrast dye to visualize the coronary arteries

Angina Complications and Outlook

In most cases, angina is due to blockages in the coronary arteries due to atherosclerosis, a buildup of cholesterol plaques. Plaque in the coronary arteries can become unstable and lead to blood clots in the coronary artery that abruptly stop blood flow to the heart, leading to a heart attack. This can be life-threatening.

Additionally, atherosclerosis in the coronary arteries means that arteries in other parts of the body are likely affected. This includes the following:

Carotid artery disease caused by atherosclerosis in the arteries in the neck, which can lead to stroke

Peripheral artery disease, caused by atherosclerosis in the leg arteries, which can impair blood flow to the legs leading to pain, and poorly healing wounds that sometimes require amputation

Intracranial atherosclerosis in the arteries in the brain that can lead to stroke

Fortunately, there are ways to decrease your risk of heart attack, stroke, and peripheral artery disease with the lifestyle changes and medical therapies discussed above.

Angina in females | 6 Warning Signs & Symptoms of Angina in females

Angina is diagnosed when a patient presents to the emergency room with a set of symptoms that alert the physician towards a possible case. These patients need several investigations to confirm the diagnosis. Therefore, anginal symptoms are the cornerstone of the diagnosis and the public should understand them as they require urgent medical consultation.

1. Chest pain or discomfort

It is by far the most common presentation of angina and one of the most common causes of admission into the ER. Causes of chest pain vary from a mild inflammation of the muscles to a rib fracture and severe life-threatening causes, which include heart attacks, pulmonary embolism (obstruction of lung arteries by blood clots), and aortic dissection (blood moving through the wall of the aorta that may rupture).

Anginal pain has a set of characteristics that make it stand out from other causes of chest pain. They are as follows:

Anginal pain is precipitated or aggravated by effort, emotional stress, or heavy meals and relieved by rest or nitroglycerin.

It feels as if pressure is exerted on the chest, or a burning sensation in the middle of the chest, or even a squeezing or a choking sensation.

Pain is usually localized just beneath the breast bone. It may also be felt in the jaw or left shoulder or down along the left arm. Anginal pain is not "Stabbing" in character, and if a stabbing pain is felt, it points towards a heart attack rather than angina, and immediate medical care is a must.

Anginal pain starts acutely and is usually relieved within 10 minutes. Therefore, chronic pain that is never relieved often excludes angina. Also, chest pain that lasts for less than 1 minute is not usually due to angina. Another type of angina is called "Angina decubitus" which occurs at night while lying down.

If anginal pain occurs at rest, it means that it progressed to unstable angina, and needs urgent medical care. Anginal pain may also be precipitated by heavy meals or cold weather. Chest pain that increases during respiration points towards causes in the chest wall itself, whether related to muscles as myositis (inflammation of muscle tissue) that may occur in influenza or bone fractures.

2. Indigestion

The chest pain in angina may be felt as a burning sensation, and it may be mistaken by many physicians as GERD, which is a condition where the acid in the stomach is "refluxed" back into the esophagus, damaging the epithelium and causing a characteristic burning sensation. Both conditions are differentiated based on medical history. While pain of angina is preceded by effort, heartburn or GERD is related to meals, and while angina is relieved by nitroglycerine, GERD is relieved by antacids. Also, investigations tests include stress ECG, and echocardiography may be needed to confirm the diagnosis. Any burning sensation in the chest, particularly if you are above 40, necessitates a visit to the doctor as soon as possible.

3. Shortness of Breath

The subjective feeling of shortness of breath is better known as "dyspnea." In these cases, the individual does not necessarily have a lack of oxygen. It is the most common symptom related to the chest along with chest pain. The causes of dyspnea range from psychological causes as panic attacks to severe causes as aspiration of foreign bodies or heart failure.

In short, if there is anything wrong in the heart, the lungs, the throat, or the nervous system, our brains may translate it into dyspnea. In the case of angina, it may result from the associated distress and feeling of impending doom, which occurs with heart attacks, or from the irregular heart rhythm that results from the heart's deprivation of oxygen.

4. Sensing your own heartbeats (palpitations)

Angina patients sometimes feel their own heartbeats, which may be distressing. We usually don't feel our own heartbeats, and if we do, it means that there is something wrong with the rhythm of our hearts, a clinical condition known as "arrhythmia." Arrhythmia may be triggered by a multitude of causes, and one of them is ischemia (decreased blood flow to the heart). When the heart can't get enough oxygen, its electrical network of fibers starts to malfunction, which eventually causes beats to be irregular.

5. Sweating

As bizarre as it sounds, sweating is an important symptom of angina and heart attacks. According to recent studies, it is suggested that profuse sweating that isn't accompanied by fever should prompt medical care for the possibility of a heart attack. The explanation for that phenomenon is that, when the body faces mortal danger -like that of a heart attack-, it triggers the sympathetic nervous system response, also known as fight or flight response, and one of its manifestations is sweating, as well as the impending sense of doom that the patient experiences along with the chest pain.

6. Fatigue and feeling of unwellness

Fatigue is a common complaint in patients suffering from heart conditions. The heart pumps blood carrying oxygen and nutrients to the body, and when this physiological process is impaired, the muscles fail to function properly because they need high and constant supply of oxygen and glucose. In the case of angina, the resulting arrhythmia and the inability of the heart to deliver the required blood to the muscles will lead to easy fatiguability and general feeling of weakness.

7. Angina in females

Although stable angina is more common in males, owing to their hormonal susceptibility to having high levels of cholesterol, and therefore a higher risk of deposition of this cholesterol and narrowing of the coronary arteries, females have a higher chance to develop other types of angina most commonly microvascular angina. Microvascular angina affects the small blood vessels that branch off the primary coronary arteries supplying the heart. This different pathology of angina causes symptoms that may be different than the classical ones discussed above, where:

Symptoms may be subtler in women, with nausea, fatigue, and a general feeling of weakness and unwellness.

Pain may be sharp rather than squeezing and may last for more than a few minutes.

Pain may occur at night or at rest and is not relieved rapidly by rest or nitrates, in contrast to the typical anginal pain.

It may be associated with other symptoms related to other diseases that commonly occur with it as migraine headaches.

How to Exercise Safely when You Have Angina

Angina, or heart pain and discomfort, occurs when your heart isn't getting an adequate supply of oxygen-rich blood. It can feel like a pain, pressure or tightness in your chest, arms, shoulders or jaw. Angina is a symptom of an underlying heart condition that's triggered when you physically exert yourself to a point where your body can not supply enough oxygen-rich blood to your heart quick enough. This could occur during exercise or even when you're walking up the stairs. However, if your angina is stable, exercise can actually improve your condition. Aerobic exercise helps improve your cardiac health and increases your circulation of that oxygen-rich blood to your heart during rest and activity. With your doctor's permission, slowly begin adding exercise safely into your weekly routine to help maintain or even improve your cardiac health.

Part1 Staying Fit if You Have Angina

Step 1

Talk to your doctor. Before starting any type of exercise program when you have chronic angina, talk to you doctor. They will be able to give you the clearance to exercise and also give you safety tips.

Before starting to exercise, ask your doctor if regular physical activity is safe and appropriate for you. Although exercise can help improve angina in many patients, this isn't true for everyone.

Ask you doctor what types of exercise are best for you. Are you allowed to do cardiovascular exercise? Should those exercises be low intensity or can you do more moderate or high intensity exercises?

Ask you doctor about what signs and symptoms are dangerous. For example, if you experience chest pain while walking on the treadmill, what should your plan of action be?

Step 2

Track your heart rate during exercise. Tracking your heart rate may be a beneficial practice when you're exercising with angina. It can give you an idea of how hard your heart is working.

Purchase a heart rate monitor for yourself. You can choose to get a wrist band or watch monitor, however it's best to purchase a chest strap monitor. These are the most accurate.

When you first start an exercise program after being diagnosed with angina, it's typically recommended to do low intensity exercises that keep your heart rate at about 50% of your maximum heart rate.

To find your maximum heart rate, subtract your age from 220. For example, if you're 60 years old, your maximum heart rate would be 160 beats per minute.

Using your heart rate tracker, keep you heart rate right at 50% during your exercise routine. In this example, you'd aim for your heart rate to be around 80 beats per minute.

If cleared by your doctor, you can slowly build up your aerobic endurance and increase to 60 or 70% of your maximum heart rate. However, don't aim to reach your max heart rate during exercise.

People with angina can adapt to exercise in a way that allows them to improve their exercise performance. Sometimes, you can take nitroglycerin to improve your exercise performance, but also, sometimes the exercise by itself helps you adapt.

Step 3

Consider starting with a cardiac rehab program. If you have been just diagnosed with angina, your doctor may suggest attending a regular cardiac rehab program. These are great medically supervised programs that can help you get back into regular exercise.

A cardiac rehab program is provided on an outpatient basis to those who have suffered from a cardiac event or have chronic cardiac conditions. They are designed to help improve fitness levels while reducing symptoms and side effects.

Talk to your doctor about going to a cardiac rehab program to help improve your aerobic endurance, physical strength and range of motion.

Stick to your cardiac rehab program until you are cleared and released for exercise on your own.

Follow up with your doctor regularly and stay on top of your cardiovascular health.

Step 4

Start with short bouts of low intensity exercises. Many people that have angina, are at lower fitness levels. This may especially be true if you've been required to take several weeks or months off from your exercise routine when you were initially diagnosed.

If you are trying to recover and rebuild your cardiac strength and endurance, it's recommended to start with short bouts of lower intensity exercises.

Restarting with higher intensity exercises, or trying to go for a longer period of time could cause symptoms to reoccur or for your condition to get worse.

Aim to start with just 15-20 minutes of low intensity activity each day. If this feels too easy, increase the time to 25-30 minutes the next day, but do not increase the intensity.

Step 5

Choose exercises that are low in intensity like walking, water walking, cycling or using the elliptical.

As your endurance gets better and your fitness improves, you can very slowly increase first the length of your exercises and then the intensity as well.

These exercises can increase your heart rate, but you are in full control of how high your heart rate increases during your exercise routine.

Always include an extended warm-up and cool-down. Warm-ups and cool-downs have always been considered an important component of any exercise routine. However, both become even more essential to safe exercise.

Slowly easing into and out of an exercise routine helps slowly increase your heart rate, blood flow and warm up your muscles. Both can also help prevent injuries.

When you have angina, warming up and cooling down your heart is essential. If you don't, you can overwork your heart too quickly which could cause an onset of symptoms.

Give your body and heart time to adjust to higher levels of activity. Start with a minimum of a 10 minute warm-up. Include very low intensity aerobic exercises and light stretching.

Also allow your heart to slowly cool down and your heart rate to slow as well. Your cool-down should also be 10 minutes of low intensity aerobic exercise followed by some light stretching.

Step 7

Avoid exercising in extreme weather conditions. Another aspect to safe exercise when you have angina is avoiding extreme weather conditions. You may be surprised how much the outdoors can effect your condition.

It's recommended to avoid exercising outdoors if it's overly cold, hot, or humid weather conditions.

Being active in these types of weather increase your risk for experiencing a cardiac event.

If you want to stay regular and consistent with exercise during more extreme weather, move your workout indoors. Walking on the treadmill, using an indoor pool or doing a aerobic DVD inside are great alternatives.

Part 2 Meeting Exercise Needs with Angina

Step 1

Start by aiming for 150 minutes of aerobic cardio each week. You may feel that because you have angina, that your total activity should be limited. However, as long as your angina is stable, you should be able to fit in about 150 minutes of cardio activity each week.

Health professionals note, that as long as your angina is stable and you have clearance from your physician, meeting the recommended activity goals each week is a safe goal.

It's recommended to aim for about 150 minutes of aerobic activity each week. Split this activity up into shorter bouts (especially if you're just starting). Try for 20 minutes 6 days a week. Or you can even do three 10 minute sessions 5 days a week.

Start with lower intensity exercises like walking or water aerobics. However, overtime, if you can, build up to more moderate intensity activities like hiking, slow jogging, using the elliptical with resistance or doing an aerobics class.

step 2

Slowly add in low intensity strength training. In addition to cardiovascular exercises, it's important to work on improving your muscular strength. Resistance or strength training will complement your aerobic work.

Health professionals also agree, that most strength training activities are also appropriate for you to do even if you have angina.

Aim to include about 20 minutes 1-2 times a week of muscle building exercises. You can try weight lifting, yoga or pilates.

Note that you my want to limit upper body exercises as these have been shown to cause angina more than lower body exercises.

step 3

Include more lifestyle activity. In addition to focusing on including more structured exercise, also increase your lifestyle activity. This is a great way for angina patients to stay active and safe.

Lifestyle activities are those exercises that you do on apart of your regular daily life. This might be walking to get the mail, taking the stairs, gardening, mowing the lawn or sweeping the floor.

They do not burn a lot of calories or spike your heart rate. However, they do keep you active and moving and elevate your heart rate mildly enough that you can still see aerobic benefits.

Many studies have shown that structured aerobic activity and increase lifestyle activity have very similar health benefits. So if you cannot do a lot of structured activity or cannot sustain activity for long, try increasing your lifestyle activity first.

step 4

Always include rest days. Although being active on a regular basis is important to regaining your aerobic strength, it's still important to include regular rest days.

Health and fitness professionals recommend that you include about one or two rest days each week. If you're just starting with exercise, you may include up to three days a week.

Rest is important for a variety of reasons. For starters, it's during rest that you improve muscle strength, see increases in muscle size and aerobic endurance.

Rest is also important for those suffering from angina because you need to allow your heart and cardiovascular system to rest and recover in between workouts.

Part 3 Staying Cautious While You Exercise

step 1

Stop if you experience any pain or discomfort.Many health professionals recommend exercise to help recover if you have angina. However, they also recommend that you be mindful of symptoms.

If you feel any type of chest pain, difficulty breathing or tightness in the chest, stop exercising immediately.

After you discontinue your exercise, keep your heart rate level low. Do not restart exercise even after the pain or other discomfort has subsided. You should take a rest day.

If you notice any pain or discomfort the following day or at your next exercise session, contact your doctor immediately.

step 2

Always carry your medications with you. There are a variety of medications that are prescribed to manage angina. Always carry these with you - especially when you're exercising.

One of the most common prescription medications that are prescribed for those with angina is nitrogen glycerin. It's to be taken when you start to experience any symptoms. This is essential to have on you at all times.

Also, make sure that others know of your condition and where your medication is. If you were to have any symptoms and couldn't get to your medications, someone else should be able to help you.

step 3

Consider bringing someone with you while you exercise. Another great idea to keep you safe during exercise, is to have someone with you. They can help treat any symptoms or serious issues that arise if you are unable to.

Although scary to think about, symptoms can occur even if you are being treated for angina. Symptoms are generally mild, but some can be more serious and life threatening.

Since exercise can precipitate symptoms, consider bringing a friend or family member with you as you exercise. They should be someone who is familiar with your condition, medications and know what to do if an emergency arises.

Try to go to the gym together, go for walks together or bike ride together. Having someone there just in case can make exercise safer and you feel more confident.

Chapter two

30 Home Remedies For Angina Symptoms (Chest Pain)

1. Garlic

Using garlic is the first treatment in this list of home remedies for angina. For thousands of years, the use of garlic not only narrowed in the kitchen space but also outreach in the prevention and treatment of some diseases.During World War II, British doctors used garlic as an antibiotic to treat wounds.Garlic has three active ingredients: allicin, liallyl sulfide and ajoene. Studies show that the essence of garlic works to strengthen the immune system, preserving the antioxidant in the body.Age, malnutrition and cigarette smoke all cause angina. They cause the aorta to harden. Regular garlic consumption slows the aging process of the aorta and helps them to become more active.

Garlic is also a very good material for diabetes patients.Garlic is always mentioned as one of the good foods for diabetics. Regular consumption of garlic also helps prevent diabetes.This is because garlic contains many nutrients that regulate blood pressure, lower cholesterol and blood sugar levels. This is a good news for diabetics.When diabetes prevention or treatment is successful, you have eliminated one of the causes of angina.

To use garlic to treat angina, besides regularly using garlic as a condiment for the dish, you can eat about 2-3 cloves of raw garlic every day.This will help you prevent and treat other illnesses like flu and sore throat.In addition, you can use garlic to relieve symptoms of angina quickly by mixing 1 teaspoon of garlic juice with a cup of warm water to drink.The pain caused by this condition will quickly disappear.

Although garlic is good, patients with hepatitis, diarrhea or kidney disease should not consume garlic on a regular basis. The active ingredients in garlic will make their condition worse.

2. Ginger

This is the next one in this list of home remedies for angina. Many people have successfully treated angina by using ginger. The reason is because ginger has the ability to prevent and treat diabetes and some other diseases. Substances in ginger can help the body avoid inflammation and swelling due to increased blood sugar. Ginger also helps reduce the risk of cardiovascular disease and protect your heart from complications such as heart attacks or coronary heart disease. Few people know that ginger can lower cholesterol and prevent blood clots. Thanks to that ability, ginger can reduce the risk of blood vessel blockage and reduce the rate of stroke due to heart disease.

Just like garlic, eating a few slices of ginger every day is what patients with angina should do. Eat ginger when your stomach is empty. In addition, a cup of warm ginger tea can help reduce the pain caused by angina. This does not take up much of your time, but the results it brings will surprise you.

The use of ginger also has some note. Although ginger is good in treating the symptoms of angina, patients should not abuse this remedy. Use ginger in moderation to get the best results.

In addition, patients with fever, hemorrhoids, liver disease, stomach pain and pregnant women should not consume ginger on a regular basis. Another thing that you need to pay attention is not to eat ginger or drink ginger tea in the evening because this is not good for your stomach.

3. Turmeric

Among home remedies for angina pain, using turmeric is one of the most effective. Turmeric is good for patients with diabetes and patients with certain blood disorders. Turmeric has the ability to reduce blood sugar and neutralize insulin, preventing diabetes. Therefore, turmeric is also referred to as one of the best foods to control diabetes. The curcumin in turmeric helps the body remove free radicals and reduce the damage to the cell membrane and DNA. Many scientific studies have shown that turmeric acts as a substance that helps cleanse the liver and improve blood circulation naturally. Therefore, turmeric can help you prevent and treat some diseases of the stomach and liver.

Digestive disorders are a disease that any age can be at risk. It causes inconvenience in daily life. Curcumin, the yellow substance of turmeric, stimulates the liver to produce and excrete bile. This helps the body improve the digestion of fat, giving you a more healthy digestive system. Besides, some of the ingredients in turmeric will help break down fat in your daily diet, helping you prevent obesity – one of the causes of angina. Because of all these reasons, the use of turmeric to treat angina is always the advice of many doctors.

To use turmeric for the purpose above, add turmeric to everyday dishes as a spice. It will increase the flavor of the dish. In addition, you can take a cup of warm turmeric tea daily to improve your situation. The way to make this tea is very simple. You only need to mix 1 teaspoon of turmeric powder with a glass of water, then boil this mixture and drink when the tea is still warm. This does not take much time but brings a lot of great results. After a period of application, you will find your angina improved, your skin is also much smoother. You can also mix turmeric powder with a glass of warm milk for daily use to get the same effect.

Although turmeric is very good, pregnant women, people with iron deficiency, patients with kidney stones and patients taking anticoagulant should not apply this remedy.

4. Cayenne Pepper

Using Cayenne pepper is the next treatment in this list of home remedies for angina symptoms. Cayenne pepper is named for the city of Cayenne (France) – where this kind of chili is grown. Cayenne pepper is usually dried, crushed and used in powder form. It is usually used as a dry spice in dishes.In particular, Cayenne pepper powder is also known as a herbal medicine to help treat some common diseases. Cayenne pepper contains many nutrients such as Vitamin A, Vitamin C, flavonoids and carotenoids, which are all pigments that work to prevent oxidation. At the same time, the hot spicy character of this kind of chili is due to the active substance capsaicin. This substance has antibacterial propery and works to help relieve pain.

A study shows that Cayenne peppers help increase body temperature. It also reduces your appetite, while promoting your body to burn more calories. As a result, one of the causes of angina – obesity – is eliminated. Cayenne peppers are also good for patients with diabetes. With this chili powder, patients with diabetes need less insulin to reduce their blood sugar.In addition, cayenne pepper also helps the heart by removing plaque from the arteries, improving blood circulation and providing the nutrients needed by the heart. Undoubtedly, Cayenne pepper is actually what patients with angina need.

To get the best results with this remedy, add the Cayenne pepper to the dish regularly. In addition, you can also mix 1 teaspoon of Cayenne pepper powder with a glass of milk or any fruit juice to reduce the pain caused by angina.

One thing to note is that breastfeeding women and people with allergies to Cayenne peppers should not apply this remedy.

5. Basil

This is one of the little-known home remedies for angina pain. Basil is a vegetable that is commonly used in everyday foods. Besides, basil also has many different healing uses. Basil contains high levels of antioxidants and essential oils that help the body produce substances such as eugenol, methy eugenol and caryphyllene. These are all substances that support normal beta cells of the pancreas (cells that store and release insulin). This improves insulin sensitivity and lowers blood sugar levels. Therefore, basil can reduce the symptoms of diabetes, including angina.

Not only good for blood sugar, basil is also very good for the heart. The antioxidant eugenol, which is abundant in basil, helps protect the heart by keeping blood pressure under control while also lowering cholesterol levels in the body. Due to its rich antioxidant properties, basil leaves are thought to help stop the development of diseases caused by smoking, including angina.

Basil has the use of anti-stress. A study conducted in India found that basil helps maintain normal levels of cortisol – the hormone that causes stress in the body. Basil leaves can soothe the nerves, regulate blood circulation and defeat free radicals – an important factor in stress. The anti-stress compounds of basil make it an ideal solution for those who want to quit smoking. Basil will soothe nerves, dispel stress – factors related to cigarette smoking. It also has the effect of cooling the throat similar to mint, which will help control cravingsfor cigarettes. As you know, stress and smoking are the causes of angina. Therefore, basil is a "savior" in your case.

The use of basil to treat angina is very simple. Chew 10-12 basil leaves when you are hungry every day, then you can get unexpected benefits. In addition, you can chew the basil when you have pain caused by angina. If you do not want to chew the basil leaves, let's drink 1 cup of basil juice every day when your stomach is empty to get the same effect. You can add honey if you want.

It is important to note that pregnant women should not consume a lot of basil because basil can have negative effects on mother and child health.

6. Alfalfa

Alfalfa is considered one of the best natural home remedies for angina pain. Alfalfa has long been known as a precious medicine because it has many effective uses in beauty and health care. For decades, Western medicine has begun to pay attention to the healing of alfalfa.

Scientists studied this herb and received positive results. Both the roots and leaves of alfalfa are useful. Alfalfa has the effect of increasing health. In addition, this herb helps to prevent anemia very effectively. It helps lower cholesterol levels and plaque buildup in the arteries, ensuring blood flow to the heart. Few people know that alfalfa leaves contain a very large amount of chlorophyll. This chlorophyll helps reduce the rate of angina.

The alfalfa is rich in saponins. Saponin is one of the common constituents of the herb, which is very beneficial for human health. Saponin is bound to bile salts and cholesterol in the intestinal tract. Bile salts form small micelles with cholesterol to facilitate its absorption. Saponin lowers blood cholesterol by preventing its re-absorption. Besides, saponin can fight the infection caused by the parasite. It also helps the immune system fight harmful bacteria. Saponins also act directly as an antioxidant, helping to reduce the risk of cancer and heart disease. Therefore, this is a remedy for angina that you should try at least once.

To use leaves for prevention or treatment of angina, drink 1-2 glasses of lukewarm alfalfa tea every day. The way to make this tea is very simple. All you need to do is mix 1-2 teaspoons dried alfalfa leaves with 1 cup of hot water, drink when the tea is still warm. Besides, you should also drink a glass of warm alfalfa tea every time the angina symptoms hurt you.

Note that patients with liver disease and pregnant women should not apply this remedy.

7. Fenugreek

The next one in this list of home remedies for angina symptoms is using fenugreek. Fenugreek is a popular herb commonly found in the Mediterranean region. However, due to its strong medicinal nature in medicine, fenugreek has become popular worldwide today.

Fenugreek helps eliminate angina by controlling diabetes. Fiber in fenugreek slows the absorption of carbohydrates and sugars of the body. In

2009, a study published in the International Journal evaluated the possibility of phenotypic hypoglycemia in patients with type 2 diabetes. This study found that 10 grams of turmeric seeds soaked in hot water could be helpful in controlling high blood sugar.

In addition, eating bread made from fenugreek powder can help reduce insulin resistance in patients with type 2 diabetes. This is really good news for people who suffer from angina due to diabetes.

As you know, high cholesterol levels are one of the causes of angina. Fenugreek is the solution to this problem because it works to lower cholesterol. It contains a large amount of soluble fiber, so it can inhibit the absorption of cholesterol and reduce the level of bad cholesterol like LDL in the body. Bad cholesterol can cause a blockage of the blood vessels leading to a heart attack or stroke. In addition, fenugreek also has antioxidant properties, which help improve cardiovascular health in general. It dilutes blood to prevent blood clots which can block blood flow to the heart, lungs and brain. In particular, fenugreek helps stabilize blood sugar and fight obesity – two major factors that increase the risk of angina. For all these reasons, the use of fenugreek for angina treatment is something you should do.

To get the great use of fenugreek, eat soaked fenugreek seeds daily. All you need to do is just soak 1 teaspoon of fenugreek seeds in water overnight. The next morning, eat them when you have not had breakfast. Also, to improve the situation quickly when angina is present, mix 1 teaspoon of fenugreek seeds with 1 cup of water, boil it for 5 minutes and then filter for water and drink. The pain will quickly be removed.

Note that people who are taking blood thinner medication should not use fenugreek to treat angina.

8. Almonds

This is one of the little-known home remedies for angina treatment. Eating almonds at a moderate level helps lower cholesterol, prevent heart disease and reduce weight. Almonds are an excellent source of vitamin E (25g almonds provide 70% of the body's daily vitamin E intake). They also contain large amounts of magnesium, potassium, zinc, fiber and iron. Besides, almonds are a healthy source of monounsaturated fats. They contain more calcium than any other nut. Therefore, they are an excellent source of food for vegetarians. Almonds also contain amygdalin (also known as laetrile or vitamin B17) which is an anti-cancer nutrient.

Almonds contain phytochemicals including beta-sisterol stigmasterol and campesterol. They are the ingredients that help you to have a healthy heart. They also have the ability to reduce the risk of heart disease by lowering LDL and cholesterol in the blood. Contains monounsaturated fats (an important fat found in the Mediterranean diet), almonds offer far greater benefits than simply lowering cholesterol.

For many years, almonds are considered nuts that can make you gain weight quickly. However, recent studies have shown that people who consume nuts tend to have lower body mass indexes. Although almonds are high in fat and calories, eating almonds at a moderate level can actually help you lose weight. As you know, obesity is one of the causes of angina. So why not try this remedy to improve this situation?

As we said above, eating almonds at a moderate level is very good. Therefore, eat about a handful of almond nuts each day. Follow this habit to get a healthy body. Besides, you can use almond oil to relieve pain. Whenever angina attacks, apply a little almond oil to your chest, the pain will quickly disappear.

Patients taking laxatives or antacids should be aware of the use of almonds. Eating almonds after about 1-2 hours after taking the medicine is the advice that the doctors give them. Eating too many almonds can make you more likely to have constipation. Therefore, please follow our guidelines for best results.

9. Omega-3 Fatty Acids

The next one in this list of home remedies for angina is Omega-3 fatty acids. Omega-3 fatty acids are essential fatty acids in the multifunctional polyunsaturated fats. Omega-3 fatty acids include Ecosapentaenoic acid (EPA) and Docosahexaenoic acid (DHA). Omega 3's EPA helps produce prostaglandin in the blood. Prostaglandins have the effect of inhibiting platelet aggregation, thereby reducing and preventing the formation of blood clots and bad cholesterol (especially triglycerides) in the blood. As a result, blood viscosity decreases, blood circulation is also improved.

Omega-3 fatty acids are essential because the body cannot synthesize them. We can only add them to the body through foods and functional foods. Omega-3 is helpful in lowering cholesterol and triglyceride levels in the blood, preventing blood clots (antithrombotic) and coronary thrombosis and helping to regulate the heart rate (antiarrhythmic). Therefore, this is a remedy for angina that you should try at least once.

Some typical Omega-3 fatty acids foods that we recommend regularly consume, such as types of seafood (especially salmon, mackerel, tuna, and shellfish), flaxseed oil, walnuts, eggs and chia seeds.

Omega-3 is a natural blood thinning agent. So, if you are taking aspirin or other anticoagulants or blood thinners, you should not increase the consumption of these foods.

10. Baking Soda

If you have angina, think of gargling with baking soda which is claimed to neutralize 70% of pathogenic bacteria, remove tonsils from the purulent accumulations, decrease pain and discomfort.

Baking soda is also known as sodium bicarbonate, which is a white non-toxic power with salty taste. This compound has the ability to treat a variety of conditions, from burns, heartburns, to acne, stomach issues, and back or chest pain, etc. You can add some baking soda to a cup of hot water, then drink this solution to release the acidity of your body, relieving chest pain naturally.

11. Brans

In order to remove cholesterol to reduce chest pain symptoms, your daily diet has to contain lots of fiber. Fortunately, bran cereal is plentiful of fiber, preventing and decreasing cholesterol from passing to your bloodstream through intestine. You just need to consume a cup of full bran cereal daily morning to get rid of chest pain.

12. Legumes And Baked Beans

One of must-try home remedies for angina is legumes or baked beans. They can support cardiovascular problems and other chest-related issues. Thanks to the high content of manganese as well as folate – two important substances for heart health, these ingredients can relieve angina symptoms if consumed at least 5 times per week.

13. Snake Gourd

This is a common herb which is potent for some maladies. Due to the rich source of minerals like iron, calcium, magnesium, oxalic acid, sodium,... snake gourd is versatile in terms of treating conditions. The leaves, roots and fruit pulp of this ingredient are usually used to deal with chest pain.

14. Soy

Being a powerhouse of proteins, calcium, dietary fiber and having low fat content, soy is one of little-known home remedies for angina. It is a great alternative for high-fat dairy products such as cheese. The proteins help to improve blood vessel system, thereby treating angina. According to some studies, it was shown that soy products can decrease the risk of cardiovascular diseases, including angina [17]. Besides, soy lecithin, which is an extract of soy oil is rich in choline, so it could help decrease cholesterol level and reduce angina pectoris. Therefore, you had better include soy to your daily diet.

15. Green Tea

This is a rich source of carbohydrate, vitamins and minerals and antioxidants. Green tea offers a number of benefits, including regulating blood pressure, decreasing pressure on artery walls, and preventing platelets from sticking. As a result, it accelerates blood flow within your body, thereby decreasing chest pain because of lack of oxygen-rich blood.

To get the best results, you are recommended to drink 3-4 cups of green tea every day. Take a cup of boiled water to dip tea bag into it. Allow it to steep for a few minutes before drinking.

16. Indian Gooseberry

This 16 is a great source of vitamin B, C, iron, phosphorus, and antioxidants. Thanks to these compounds, you can use Indian Gooseberry for some heart illnesses. Also, Indian gooseberry also helps to maintain proper cholesterol level within the body, prevent the buildup of plaque – one of primary reasons for chest pain and angina.

You can take advantage of Indian gooseberry in the form of juice, powder, or raw.

17. Celery And Carrot Juice

Carrots have a rich content of vitamin A and beta-carotene, helping to boost the immunity and decrease cholesterol levels. Carrots and celery are also plentiful of potassium and iron. Thus, it is a wonderful detox concoction that purifies your blood. Also, it strengthens the heart muscles as well as arterial valves and alkalizes blood stream.

You can prepare the fresh juice of carrot or celery to take their advantage.

18. Grapes

Another natural home treatment among home remedies for angina is grapes, which is a rich source of vitamin C and has strong antioxidants. It can decrease inflammation, boost blood flow, and improve heart health. Thus, it can cure and prevent angina.

You can eat grapes or take advantage of grape seed extract to lower the risk of heart diseases, including angina.

19. Grapefruit

Grapefruits are not grapes, but they are all good cures for angina. Grapefruits are rich in magnesium, which is an important mineral for angina. You had better consume this fruit every day. However, be careful if you are taking any kind of tablet for cardiovascular issues.

20. Oregano Oil

Among home remedies for angina, oregano oil is lesser-known but works well. This oil contains antifungal and antibacterial properties, so it helps to take control of respiratory issues and decrease chest pain. If the reason of your chest pain is respiratory problems, then oregano oil is your solution. It has carvacrol, flavonoids, rosmarinic acid, terpenes, and acts as anti-histamines and decongestants. Therefore, oregano oil can decrease chest pain due to respiratory tract infections. The anti-histamines in oregano oil can prevent plaque buildup in arteries, which is a result of chest pain, not to mention the ability of preventing cold and coughs that cause chest pain.

You can take oregano oil in a few ways for angina treatment:

You can inhale oregano oil's scent before your bedtime to get rid of chest pain.

Combine 10-12 drops of oregano oil with any essential oil such as jojoba oil, then massage it onto your chest area.

Mix 2-3 drops of oregano oil with a cup of water, have it once per day.

21. Tomato

Tomatoes is rich in vitamin A, C, E, lycopene, beta-carotene, folic acid, and so on. They are good for heart health by reducing the risk of heart strokes, deoxidizing LDL – the "bad" cholesterol. Therefore, you should consume tomatoes daily to prevent and treat angina pain.

22. Pomegranate Juice

Pomegranate juice is beneficial for cardiovascular diseases, including angina. It can reduce oxidative stress and prevent the arteries from being damaged. At the same time, this fruit can help with synthesis of nitric oxide and prevent LDL from ruining your heart. Drink pomegranate juice to clear fatty acid deposits, thereby opening up your arteries. Pomegranate juice is supposed to have equal effects on both females and males and could relieve chest pain.

23. Apple Cider Vinegar

With amazing properties, apple cider vinegar can actively kill of the bacterial responsible for mucus production in chest, thereby relieving chest pain. Also, apple cider vinegar can ease breathing, decrease chest pain caused by acid reflux. The acetic acid of vinegar can decrease stomach acidity, maintains pH level within your body, thereby limiting the risk of chest pain in the years to come.

24. Licorice Root

Generally used to prepare Ayurvedic medicine, licorice root can help with diarrhea and stomach issues and chest pain. Some people take licorice by mouth for bronchitis, sore throat, cough, and some infections caused by viruses and bacteria. This herb is rich in flavonoids, helping to flush your body from toxins and open up the arteries for appropriate blood flow.

Make licorice root tea by adding licorice root powder in boiling water, let it steep for a few minutes before straining. Sip it slowly. To sweeten it, add some honey. It is best to drink 1-2 cups of this tea every day.

25. Peanut Butter

You will find a rich content of monounsaturated fats in peanut butter, which helps to decrease LDL – the "bad" cholesterol – in the blood and improve good HDL – the "good" cholesterol" – in your body. Also, it assists in maintaining blood vessel and heart health.

Take 1 tablespoon of unsalted and fat-free peanut butter no less than 5 times per week to reap its benefits. In case peanut butter is unavailable or if you are not a fan of it, then take 2 tablespoons of peanuts every day as an alternative.

26. Ginkgo Biloba

Gingko biloba can boost the supply of oxygen-rich blood. It is a powerhouse of antioxidants, so it helps to eradicate free radical damages. This herb is helpful for not only angina but also cardiovascular problems. You could consume 80 mg of gingko Biloba for 3 times per day to harness its benefits.

27. Sprirulina

This is a cardio prective agent which can prevent and decrease the deposite of low-density lipids because of the availability of gamma linoleic acid (GLA). There are 18 proteins presenting in this small ingredient, which are a rich source of vitamin B12, E, zinc, manganese, copper and so on. It can control the cholesterol levels, so helping to treat some heart diseases. Consume it as a supplement with the supervision of your doctor.

28. Artichoke

This is a good solution for heart diseases, including angina. It is thanks to its glycemic and lipidic-reducing actions. It assists in reducing blood pressure as well as cholesterol levels. Furthermore, this herb can control some diseases which result in angina.

Infuse 2 tablespoons of dried artichoke leaves in about 1 liter of water. Have this drink 3 times per day before having meals.

Besides, you can also mix green artichoke leaves with wine if the dried leaves are unavailable.

29. Parsley

It is one of the best home remedies for angina pain along with other cardiovascular diseases. You could consume fresh parsley leaves or as a natural herb. Make a tea from fresh parsley leaves by adding ¼ cup of its leaves to 1 cup of boiling water. After 10 minutes of steeping, strain it. Then, drink this tea 1-2 times per day for optimal results.

30. Yoga Poses

People who feel an ache in their chest area may not necessarily suffer from cardiovascular disease. It could be, of course. When the human heart does not get adequate oxygen, it will increase the risk of chest pain, also called angina. In such case, you can practice some yoga poses to relieve angina pain. Yoga helps to reduce chest tightness by opening, expanding and stretching the human chest. Also, it assists in improving your motion range, stretching pectoral muscles, and boosting flexibility, which help to eliminate chest pain.

Some of the most recommended yoga poses of chest pain relief are:

Matsyasana

This pose is also called as fish pose which is a beginner level of Hatha yoga asana. You are advised to practice this pose in the morning before having a breakfast to have best results. Or, it may be good to take a rest of several hours between the exercise and your last meal. This will help you have enough time to digest foods well. However, after all, this exercise should be practice in the morning. By practicing this yoga pose, you will stretch your chest as well as neck areas, relese shoulder and neck tension, alleviate respiratory problems, tone the parathyroid, pineal glands and pituitary, and stretch and tone your back.

Lie on your back, legs together and hands placed on sides

Place the palms down and under the hips

Bring your elbows close to one another and place them close to the waist

Cross legs with legs cross one another at the middle of your body

Maintain your knees and thighs flat on the ground

Breathe in, raise your chest up with head lifted and crown touching the ground

Move all of your weight on your elbows so that you feel lightly pressure on shoulder blades

Keep this position till you can bear with normal breath

Exhale, then release this position, lift your head and drop your chest to the ground

Untangle the legs before relaxing

Do this exercise from 30 to 60 seconds

Ustrasana

This pose also has another named as Camel Pose. It resembles a camel's stance. It is recommended to practice in the morning before having a breakfast. Ustrasana helps to stretch and strengthen the back as well as shoulder. Also, it opens the chest while improving respiration. Practicing this pose will help tone your neck while stretching your throat.

Steps to take:

Kneel on the floor with hands on hips

Maintain your knees in lined with the shoulders and foot soles face the roof

Then, inhale and draw the tailbone in towards the pubis so that you feel a pull at the navel

Whilst doing so, arch the backs

Slide the palms over the feet, straighten the arms

Try to keep your neck in a neutral pose for 30-60 seconds prior to releasing

You had better avoid this yoga pose in case of having a neck or back injury. If you have low or high blood pressure, insomnia, or migraines, then do not do this asana.

Bhujangasana (Cobra Pose)

This is also called as Cobra pose which is a beginner level Ashtanga yoga asana. Similar to the first pose, you should also practice this pose in the morning before eating anything.

This exercise will stretch your chest and shoulder muscles, increase your flexibility and boost your mood. Also, it improves your oxygen and blood circulation.

What you have to do:

Lie flat with stomach down, hands on sides and toes touching one another

Move the hands to your front side, placed at shoulder level and palms down on the floor

Place all of your body weight on palms, inhale, raise the trunk and head with your arms bent at the elbows

Arch the neck backward so that it replicates the cobra with raised hood.

Keep the shoulders away from the ears and shoulder blades firm

Press the thighs, hips and feet to the ground

Keep this position for 15-30 seconds whilst breathing

Bring the hands back to your sides, your head rested with forehead contacting with the ground.

Place hands under the head and rest your head slowly on one of your side. Breathe

With this pose, you will feel stomach pressed against the ground. You should avoid practicing it if you are suffering from hernia, headaches, pregnancy, back injuries, carpal tunnel syndrome, and abdominal surgeries.

Dhanurasana

Also called as bow pose, this exercise is a beginner level of Vinyasa yoga asana. It should be also practiced in the morning before eating anything. This pose is one of the 3 major back stretching exercises. It massages your heart, treats your asthma, and relieves fatigue and stress while opening up your chest, shoulders and neck.

All you have to do is:

Lie flat with stomach down on the floor, feet hip-width apart and arms on your sides

Fold the knees and keep your ankles gently

After inhaling, lift the chest and legs off the floor, legs pulled back

Look straight and smile

Keep this pose while focusing on your breath

After 15-20 seconds, exhale and release this pose

Avoid this exercise if you are suffering from headaches, hernia, lower back pain, neck injuries, low or high blood pressure, and abdominal surgeries. Pregnant women should avoid this exercise also.

Chakrasana

The last but not least effective yoga pose for angina relief is called wheel pose. This pose requires practitioners perform the shape like a wheel. Practicing this pose will be good for your heart, cure your asthma, stretch your lungs, and boost your thyroid. It also helps with depression and relieves tension and stress in the human body.

All you have to do is:

Lie on the floor with your back down with hip-width apart

Bend the knees so that foot soles are on the mat and closer to the buttocks

Hands placed behind the shoulders, fingers opened up and directed towards the shoulders

Balance the weight on the limbs, press your palms and feet while lifting your body off the floor

Allow your head to hang lightly and keep your neck long

Take deep, slow breaths and keep this position for about 1 minute until you can't stand

Release this pose by bending the legs and arms

Lower your back gently on the mat and lie down for several minutes

This pose should be avoided if you have carpal tunnel syndrome, tendonitis, lower back pain, high blood pressure, headaches or shoulder impingement.

Bitilasana

Aka cow pose, Bitilasana is similar to the exercises above in terms of exercising conditions. It improves your balance and posture, strengthens your neck, stretches your back, calms your mind and relieves stress. Besides, it boosts blood circulation within your body.

Start with knees placed under the hips, wrists are lined with your shoulders

Keep your head hang in a neutral position, gaze softly at the ground

After inhaling, life the buttocks upwards when you open the chest. Allow your stomach sink towards the floor. Lift the head while looking towards the ceiling

Keep this position for several seconds, breathe out and return to the initial position

Do this exercise for 5-6 times

Note: People with neck injury should consult their doctor before practicing this exercise.

Natarajasana

Natarajasana is also called as Dance pose which stretches the neck muscles while strengthening the chest. Practicing it will help you improve your flexibility and boost the balance of your body. You should practice it before having a breakfast.

Take the steps below:

Stand in the pose of Tadasana

Breathe in while lifting the left foot with the heel placed towards the left buttock and knees bent

Put your whole body weight on the right foot

Push the ball of your right thigh bone into your hip joint

After that, pull your kneecap up in order to keep your standing leg straight and strong

With torso upright, use your left hand to grasp your left foot from the outside. Do not compress your lower back. Let your pubis lifted towards the navel while pressing the tailbone to the ground

Start to raise the left foot up and away from your torso, your back and the floor as well

Extend your left thigh behind your back and parallel to the ground with the right arm stretched forwards

Keep this position for 15-30 seconds before releasing

Repeat on your other side

Note: Do not practice this exercise if you have low blood pressure.

Some Attention

Here are some things to keep in mind during the course of treatment:

Reduce stress – one of the causes of angina. You can join a yoga or meditation class to improve the situation.

If your condition is due to obesity, let's exercise and establish a proper diet to lose weight.

Limit alcohol, beer and cigarettes.

Eat slowly, do not eat and work at the same time.

Use vegetable oils for cooking such as coconut oil and olive oil.

Limit strong sports and strenuous activities.

Above are home remedies for angina treatment. These are all very simple and effective ways. They are all tested ways, so you can fully trust their safety. Let's get rid of the symptoms of angina by applying them today. If you have any contributing ideas about our article of "Top 30 Natural Home Remedies For Angina Symptoms (Chest Pain)" introduced in Home Remedies Category, do not hesitate to drop your words below this post. We will answer as soon as we could.

CHAPTER THREE

CONCLUSION

Angina is a serious condition related to impaired blood flow to the heart causing chest discomfort. The primary cause is atherosclerosis or cholesterol plaques in the coronary arteries. It increases risk of heart attack, and is associated with blockages in other arteries that can increase risk of stroke.

Printed in Great Britain
by Amazon

29126580R00056